For June, with love

Text and illustrations copyright © Graham Marsh 2009, 2014

The rights of Graham Marsh to be identified as the author and illustrator of this Work
has been asserted by him in accordance with the Copyright, Designs and Patent Act, 1988.

First published in Great Britain and in the USA in 2009.
This early reader edition first published in Great Britain and in the USA in 2014 by
Frances Lincoln Children's Books, 74-77 White Lion Street, London N1 9PF
www.franceslincoln.com

Acknowledgements
A tip of the beret to: Ben Shahn, David Stone Martin and Terry Southern.

Also the following cats must get theirs: John Gall, Joakim Olsson, Glyn Callingham,
Sam the Cat, June Marsh, Jack Cunningham, Max and Coco Katz, Tony Nourmand,
The Crew from the Island, Nicole and Tony Crawley, Janetta Otter-Barry, Judith Escreet,
Yvonne Whiteman, David Cutts and Richard Riddick.

A CIP catalogue record for this book is available from the British Library.

978-1-84780-544-7

Printed in China

1 3 5 7 9 8 6 4 2

MAX AND THE LOST NOTE

WRITTEN AND ILLUSTRATED BY
GRAHAM MARSH

F
FRANCES LINCOLN
CHILDREN'S BOOKS
www.franceslincoln.com

This is Max. He is a cat who plays piano. Max is a
sharp dresser. Some cats say he is as dapper as
Dan and hip as Harry.

That means he is a very cool cat indeed.

One day Max was writing a new tune when suddenly
he stopped . . .

Max had lost one of his notes, and could not finish
the tune.

Max looked everywhere for his lost note.
He looked right. He looked up. He looked left.

He even looked in the suitcase which he kept in his room. "I know. I'll see if any of the other cats have found my lost note," thought Max.

So Max rode his scooter downtown . . . stopping at
Kitty's Place for a glass of milk and some catnip.
At Kitty's he met The Felines.

The Felines were a famous vocal group. There were Florence, Phoebe, Ella and Coco. They wore groovy clothes and were always singing.

Max asked The Felines to sing for him. Perhaps his lost note was hidden in one of their songs.
No luck. The note was not there. Then Coco said, "Try Long Tall Dexter. He has plenty of notes."

Max told Long Tall Dexter about his lost note. "Let me see," said Dexter. "I will play something for you on my saxophone and we will see if it is there."

When he had finished playing, Max said, "That's a
cool tune, Dexter, but my lost note isn't there."
"Now listen, Max, my furry little friend," said Dexter.
"I know three cats called Miles, Oliver and Charlie
who might just know where your lost note is."

"Tell them Long Tall Dexter sent you."
It was a warm sunny day. Max decided to walk.
So, he left his scooter and his jacket at
Dexter's house.

Max met up with Dexter's cats. There was Miles who played trumpet, Oliver who was a drummer and Charlie who played a mean guitar.

They played some funky music for Max . . . but his
lost note was not there.

Max was beginning to think he would never find his lost note. Then he saw his neighbour Rita sitting on a bench. She was playing her flute.

She asked, "What happened, Max?"

"I have lost a note," said Max.

"Is it this one?" Rita asked, and she played a beautiful song on her flute.

"I wish it was," said Max. "That was sweet."

Suddenly Rita had a thought.
"Go and see my friend Sam," she said.
"He has a new double bass. It is so big, your
missing note might just have landed there."

Now Sam, like Max, was a very cool cat indeed.
He had a different hat for every day of the week.
That is seven hats.

The notes coming from Sam's double bass made
Max feel very sleepy. Max said, "I like your music
very much, Sam. But my lost note isn't there."

Max walked home. On the way he listened to the sounds of the city, the birds, the cars, the buses, even the fat cat selling newspapers.

There was music in everything, if you took time to listen. But Max could not hear his lost note.

When Max got home, he sat down and kicked off his shoes. Suddenly, he saw something that made him nearly jump out of his seat.

There, stuck to the sole of one shoe, was his lost
note! He must have stepped on it while he was
writing his new tune.

Max thought the note was not lost after all.
It was just missing!

Now Max could finish his tune. All the cats joined in, and they sang and played for hours.

Max was one happy cool cat.

Collect the TIME TO READ books:

978-1-84780-476-1

978-1-84780-475-4

978-1-84780-477-8

978-1-84780-478-5

978-1-84780-543-0

978-1-84780-544-7

978-1-84780-542-3

978-1-84780-545-4

Frances Lincoln titles are available from all good bookshops.
You can also buy books and find out more about your favourite titles,
authors and illustrators on our website: www.franceslincoln.com